Father and Son

DENIZÉ LAUTURE

illustrated by JONATHAN GREEN

PHILOMEL BOOKS • NEW YORK

A NOTE ABOUT THIS BOOK:

Father and Son is set in the low country of South Carolina, the home of the Gullah people. Some of the scenes I've painted in the book may not be familiar to readers but are part of Gullah life.

The picture of the father and son carrying wood on their heads is something you can see three times a day, as men, women, and children carry pieces of wood and branches in this way to use as fuel in old wood-burning stoves.

Sweet-potato huts are still used today by people of the low country for storage and protection of sweet potatoes and yams. The huts are always cylindrical in shape and made out of pine straw, cornstock, and soil. – J. G.

Each illustration in this book is an oil painting, which was photographed for transparency, scanned by laser, and then reproduced in full color.

The artist gratefully acknowledges the help of Tim Stamm in making the transparencies of the artwork for this book.

PHILOMEL BOOKS
A division of Penguin Young Readers Group.
Published by The Penguin Group.
Penguin Group (USA) Inc., 375 Hudson Street, New York, NY 10014, U.S.A.
Penguin Group (Canada), 90 Eglinton Avenue East, Suite 700, Toronto, Ontario M4P 2Y3, Canada (a division of Pearson Penguin Canada Inc.).
Penguin Books Ltd, 80 Strand, London WC2R 0RL, England.
Penguin Ireland, 25 St. Stephen's Green, Dublin 2, Ireland (a division of Penguin Books Ltd).
Penguin Group (Australia), 250 Camberwell Road, Camberwell, Victoria 3124, Australia (a division of Pearson Australia Group Pty Ltd).
Penguin Books India Pvt Ltd, 11 Community Centre, Panchsheel Park, New Delhi - 110 017, India.
Penguin Group (NZ), 67 Apollo Drive, Rosedale, North Shore 0632, New Zealand (a division of Pearson New Zealand Ltd).
Penguin Books (South Africa) (Pty) Ltd, 24 Sturdee Avenue, Rosebank, Johannesburg 2196, South Africa.
Penguin Books Ltd, Registered Offices: 80 Strand, London WC2R 0RL, England.

Library of Congress Cataloging-in-Publication Data
Lauture, Denize, 1946–
Father and son / Denize Lauture ; illustrated by Jonathan Green.
Summary: A father and son in the low country of South Carolina share special feelings as they spend time together in a variety of activities.
1. Fathers and sons—Juvenile poetry. 2. Children's poetry, American. I. Green, Jonathan, 1955– ill. II. Title.
PS3562.O793 F37 2009
811'.54—dc22
2009464758

ISBN 978-0-399-21867-5
Special Markets ISBN 978-0-399-25492-5 Not for resale
1 3 5 7 9 10 8 6 4 2

To all children who show great respect and love
to every decent man they meet down the many roads of life.
To all men who understand they must love, adopt,
and give a hand to all children of our poor planet.
And to my children, Charles and Conrad.
—D.L.

I am dedicating this book to my patrons, collectors,
and supporters, and to my family for instilling in me a rich
cultural heritage that serves as the genesis for many
of my paintings.
—J.G.

Father and son
Hand in hand
Up on the road
In the sun,

Their bodies stop
The same breeze,

Bend the same sun rays,

And sway left and right,
And right and left,
At the same time.

They gaze
At the same fruit tree,

Listen
To the same bird song,

And hum
The same melody.

They swing together
The same arm,
Land together
The same foot,

And follow together
The same cloud,
Measuring the same ground.

The shadow of one
Touching
The shadow of the other,

The mind of one
Sparking
The mind of the other,

The heart of one
Reaching out to
The heart of the other,

And the soul of one
Knowing
The soul of the other,

Down the road
In the sun,
Father and son
Hand in hand.